Disney's HERCULES

Adapted by Justine Korman

Illustrated by Peter Emslie and Don Williams

ADAPTED FROM
WALT DISNEY PICTURES' **HERCULES**
MUSIC BY ALAN MENKEN LYRICS BY DAVID ZIPPEL ORIGINAL SCORE BY ALAN MENKEN
PRODUCED BY ALICE DEWEY AND JOHN MUSKER & RON CLEMENTS
DIRECTED BY JOHN MUSKER & RON CLEMENTS

A GOLDEN BOOK • NEW YORK

Golden Books Publishing Company, Inc., Racine, Wisconsin 53404

Long ago, the Earth was ruled by monsters called Titans.
Then a mighty god named Zeus locked the Titans away
beneath the ocean so that he and his fellow gods and
goddesses could rule the world from Mount Olympus.

One happy day, Zeus's wife, Hera, gave birth to a very strong baby. She named him Hercules. All the gods gathered to celebrate the birth.

And, as a gift, Zeus gave his son a flying horse called Pegasus.

Hades, the evil god of the Underworld, was among the guests that day. When he left the celebration, he returned to his dark domain and met his two demon helpers, Pain and Panic. Hades was on his way to a meeting with the three Fates.

Hades had a plan to take over Olympus, but he wanted to know if it would succeed. So he asked the Fates, three sisters who shared one eye—an eye that saw the past, present, and future.

In eighteen years, the planets would line up, the Fates said, and Hades could then defeat Zeus by releasing the Titans. "But," the Fates warned, "should Hercules join the fight, you will fail."

So Hades decided to get rid of Hercules. He sent his helpers, Pain and Panic, to steal the baby. They took him to Earth and forced him to drink a magic potion—one that would change him from a god to a human.

But before the last drop was drunk, a kindly couple—
Amphitryon and Alcmene—came along.

Pain and Panic turned themselves into deadly snakes
in order to complete their task, but the snakes were no
match for Hercules' amazing strength!

"Perhaps the gods have finally answered our prayers for a child," Alcmene said, as she looked at the medallion the baby wore.

The couple decided to raise Hercules as their own child.

Zeus and Hera missed their son, but only gods could live on Olympus. And Hercules was no longer a god.

As young Hercules grew up, he was always kindhearted, eager to be helpful—and very accident-prone.

One day, he accidentally destroyed the whole marketplace!
"Hercules is dangerous!" cried one of the merchants.
"He didn't mean any harm," Amphitryon said.
But the townspeople shouted, "Keep that freak away from here!"

"Where do I belong?" Hercules wondered. At last it was time for Amphitryon and Alcmene to tell him how he'd been found and to show him the medallion he had been wearing.

"It's the symbol of the gods," Alcmene explained.

"The gods!" Hercules cried. "Maybe they know where I belong."

In search of an answer, Hercules visited the temple of Zeus. As Hercules prayed to the statue of Zeus, it came to life. Zeus told Hercules all about his beginnings. Then he said, "If you prove yourself a true hero on Earth, you will be a god again."

"How do I become a hero?" Hercules asked.

Zeus told Hercules to go find Philoctetes, the trainer of heroes. Zeus whistled for Pegasus, the flying horse he had given Hercules years before, and Pegasus flew Hercules to Phil's island home.

"I'm out of the hero business," Phil told Hercules. "I'm sick of losers." But when he learned that Hercules was Zeus's son, Phil changed his mind.

Hercules trained hard. Finally he told Phil, "I'm ready to battle monsters, rescue damsels—you know, heroic stuff."

Phil agreed. "Saddle up, kid. We're going to the big city of Thebes," he said.

On the way, Hercules rescued a girl named Megara from a centaur. Hercules didn't know it, but Meg was mixed up with Hades.

And Hades had a plan. He forced Meg to trick Hercules into fighting the Hydra, a monster with many heads.

Just when it seemed as if Hercules were doomed, he smashed his mighty fists into a cliff. With a great crash, the whole cliff tumbled down onto the Hydra. Hercules won!

So Hades set an even trickier trap—he ordered Meg to become friendly with Hercules. "Find out his weakness and I'll set you free," he added.

Meg tried, but instead of finding Hercules' weakness, she fell in love with him—and he with her.

When Hades realized how much Hercules cared for Meg, he made her his hostage. Then he told Hercules, "Give up your strength for the next twenty-four hours and no harm will come to her."

Hercules could not let anything bad happen to Meg, so he agreed.

Now, after eighteen long years, Hades' plan was poised for success. The planets were lined up in the proper order, just as the Fates had predicted. And Hercules was helpless!

Hades released the Titans from their prison. As soon as they were free, the terrible Titans stormed Olympus!

At the same time, Hades sent the giant Cyclops to attack
Thebes and kill Hercules!

"Hercules! Save us!" the people cried.

Meg warned Hercules that without his strength he'd be
killed, but someone had to stand up to the Cyclops.
Hercules grabbed a burning stick to fight the monster.

After the Cyclops fell off a cliff, Meg pushed Hercules out of the way of a falling column, and the column fell on her instead. Because Meg was injured, the deal with Hades was broken, and Hercules suddenly had his strength back. He lifted the huge column off Meg easily.

"Hurry! You can still stop Hades," Meg urged.

Hercules flew straight to Olympus to free his father and the other gods. Hercules joined forces with them and defeated the Titans.

He then hurried back to Meg's side. But it was too late—her spirit had disappeared into the Underworld.

But Hercules was determined to save Meg. So he traveled to the Underworld in order to bring Meg's spirit back to the world of the living.

"That's impossible—unless you're a god," Hades fumed.

It had happened at last! By risking his own life for Meg, Hercules had become a true hero and had earned his place on Olympus once more.

But Hercules chose not to stay above the clouds. He had
finally found the place where he belonged—on Earth, with
Meg. From that day forward, Hercules lived happily and well,
and his brave deeds were written in the stars.